# 3 Women on The Cusp

**By Jo Aldred : Lindsay Dowding : Lynn Rutherford**

**Published by Cusp Publishing in 2008**
**42 Queen's Street, Spooner Row, Norfolk NR18 9JU**
**www.cusppublishing.co.uk**



**ISBN 978-0-9560834-0-1**

Printed and bound in Great Britain by Dynamic Impressions Ltd.

Dear Reader,

We hope you have as much enjoyment reading our book, as we did, creating it. For your guidance, a "coding" system, to support your reading, has been provided!!!

Advisory Coding System - Key.

Sobriety - Read sober, in full control of faculties.

Fortification - Fortify yourself, to aid enjoyment.

Lubrication - To let your mind run free.

Intoxication - To excite the senses.

Inebriation - Who cares anyway!

We think it important to say that these jottings cover the last 25 years. They were often inspired by times of transition. They are very personal and it's not always easy to share....however, we encouraged each other and we hope you, 'Dear Reader' might do the same.

... Acknowledgements ...

...Photos of the 3 of us, including cover shots ... by Anna Hirst ...assisted by Teresa Dowding..

...Typing, layout, organising people and paper! ... by Lindsay Dowding ..

...Other photos and drawing for "French Story" ... by Jo Aldred ...

... Drawings and photos for "Where you are" and "Earth" ... by Lynn Rutherford ..

...[Husbands photos: by wives!]..

...For regular use of the "Agricultural Bar"...
in "the Boars" ~ Spooner Row ~
for our "Office" ~
Our thanks to Tony & Ruth...

....thanks also to our printer Barney for his enthusiasm, humour and excellent coffee!

# Index

# THREE WOMEN

Lynn

Three women on the cusp we are
Our hormones faileth daily
With hope we wish upon a star
And smile at life more gaily

Our friendships made in music were
Alto and two sopranos
We trilled and cooed and laughed and sighed
Around an old 'piaano'

Now, moved to write and sing and draw
Exploring life's big riddles
We sup some lovely wine until…
We really get quite piddled!

Whichever stage of life YOU'RE at
Your youth or your maturity
Enjoy your friends like we three do
And aim for perpetuity!!

I had an interesting and unusual childhood and, lurching towards middle age decided that I did not want my life and experiences to disappear into oblivion. I decided to write down the moments that had left their mark on me; the moments that had made me the person I was now.
I was on a coach driving through night to the Czech Republic to sing Mozart's Requiem in Prague and had taken a note book with me in case of inspiration.
A signpost to Ypres brought memories flooding back.
I took out the note book and began to write. Jo.

## THE GATE

Driving along the road to Armentier, a signpost to Ypres and the Menin Gate reminds me that this is one I must write about.

Dad worked for a well known charity and he spent most of my childhood travelling Europe visiting refugee camps and raising money by preaching with his exhibition 'Operation Hope', in almost every Anglican Church on the continent. In the school holidays my mother, brother and I travelled with him.
We saw sights, met people and heard stories that meant our lives were entwined with those who lived in post-war Europe in poverty in tin shacks, stateless, bereaved, memories full of their past and yet, so very often, with hope for the future.

8.00 p.m. Silence, a dark night, no traffic - all stopped. Emotion I didn't understand.

Mum and Dad wanted to make sure we drove through Ypres on our way home.
What year? I can't remember at the moment, late 50s, early 60s? I'm not sure. I think it was raining, it was dark.
I hadn't known what to expect.
We drove along a main street; probably, at that time, one of the few G.B. vehicles around, (people didn't go on foreign holidays in the same way that they do now).
I think we stopped a few minutes before 8.00 p.m.
Mum and Dad got out, fine drizzle now. Did I get out? I think so.
I see wet on the cobbled street, the reflections of street lamps shimmering.
The sound of cars, lorries (very few), drawing to a halt, switching off engines.
Unknown people standing, heads bowed, silence.

Had even the dogs stopped barking?
A lone bugler stepping out into the middle of the road, as one had only a few years before on the evening Ypres was liberated and fighting was still going on in some of the town's streets.
No fuss, no fanfare in the damp air, no tourists, no cameras; only silence.

Just the local people stopping as usual. And us.
What did he play? The Last Post? I believe it was.
A volunteer from the local fire brigade.
Haunting, alone, full of pride, proud to be able to stand there and show his respect for those who had died protecting his town and those who had died liberating it…and defiance?
Not a tourist attraction then, only a simple act of remembrance in a small town that most people in England at that time seemed to know little about.

Mum and Dad moved to tears, silent, gently watering eyes; so heartfelt. They knew what it meant, they could remember.
My brother and I, did we remember? No, we had no such memory; we only knew what we had been told but we felt the emotion, the silent sigh, the beating hearts of those who stopped each day on their way out in the evening, or just if they were passing on that street at that time.
We felt the dignity and the silent respect for those who had given their lives; so many of them.
Then moments of silence and he was gone into the dark.

Cars started up and moved on, people carried on walking as if they hadn't stopped, finished off conversations that had halted mid-sentence a few minutes earlier.
Not because they didn't care, but because this was part of their daily lives.
An act of simple remembrance, ever present.
No fuss, no need to discuss it - just the need to stop and remember.

Mum and Dad got back into the van.
We drove away in silence.

Written in Aldeburgh 2006 after a lovely walk with my Mum. Lynn

## ALLOTMENTS

Broad beans, furry leaved, bee flowered,
Crowding the cabbage, pleated, crimped
Pearly green, welcome the arrivals…
Mostly men of a certain age, (some women)
Arrive on sturdy bicycles, armed with flasks.

First, their nostrils are assaulted
By the heavenly perfume of sweet peas
Dancing and tapping at their lattice of green string at the side
Of the sheds, or between the rhubarb and the potatoes.
How their mouths water at the thought
Of their gathering in the fruits of their labours from
This little patch of earth.

They will roll the beans around until
They puncture, nutty on the tongue.
The potatoes, tiny, earthy floury morsels
Harvested before their time -
The children of the allotment.
Runner beans, bright red,
As pretty to see as good to eat.
The sun's good light deepening their green
Strengthening the sinews of those who devour them greedily.
Only really exquisite in their season.

The Marigolds and Poppies brightly wave their greetings,
The small Chrysanths, waiting for cooler weather,
Growing up to take their places.
We know that they and the Dahlias will fill the late summer air
With the promise of autumn and cooler winds across the marshes.
Bright butterflies, bees, join the dots between all this bounty.

The mind of the gardener, the allotment tender,
The hands calloused, that prune and plant and coax and harvest
Are in tune. A gently English tune,
Woven into the brown earth with serenity, contentment
And a knowledge of time passing,
Of the seasons and the opportunity
To shape the land with growing things
And taste the jewels in the garden through mouth and breath and touch.

*Before we were married, John and I had a holiday in Greece - neither of us had been there before. We arrived at the apartment early in the morning, cold and tired after a night time of travelling. We went to bed and slept until the sun woke us streaming through the shutters. We got up, made breakfast and sat out on the terrace planning our days to come. I wrote about some of the days in the evenings, unless overtaken by too much tiredness or red wine. Lindsay*

## NOTES FROM A JOURNEY TO KIMI.

We are nearly at the end of our stay in Greece and have become well used to the vagaries of our apartment. Don't get me wrong, it's a lovely simple apartment, white walls and tiles, fluffy blue blankets and a secluded balcony overlooking citrus trees and an olive grove but we have gradually customised it to our needs during our short time here.
The absent bathroom sink plug was soon dealt with… a left over foil-containered butter pat from Olympic Airlines proved a perfect substitute. A candle makes an excellent bedside lamp for late reading and even the ever-changing solar-heated hot water system seemed to take on some sort of recognisable pattern. Certain unalterables remain; the mattress/palliasse with strange, hard ridges, and the whistling kettle which alerts us to when the water is boiling by shooting the 'whistle' off so that it hits the wall opposite!
Anyhow, yesterday, as ever, the sun shone out of a clear blue sky, streaming through the softly draped curtains to wake us and so we decided to set off in the hire car in an easterly direction, heading for Avlonari…a hilltop village with a huge Lombard tower at the very top.
First we passed through Amarynthos, next along the coast from Eretria. I noticed that they had poor, thin, pimply, plucked chickens hanging from the shop doorways, usually just one per shop, dangling over the cars as they hooted and manoeuvred their way on the busy road. Did people buy the poor solitary chicken or was it a sort of advertisement for fresher chickens within? Did the shopkeeper leave it hanging there until it became too battered and disreputable and then replace it? I had wondered this with the octopus tentacles which hung quite routinely outside the Tavernae but then noticed that they were definitely taken down and used for cooking. I felt sad for the chicken though not for the octopus, which is rather unfair.
We left Amarynthos behind, passed through Aliveri, turned left at Lepoura and soon arrived at Hani Avlonariou hoping to see the 14th century Basilica of Ayios Dimitrios…'locked but ask for the key at the café next door' the guidebook said.

It transpired that there was no café next door and the proprietor of the café opposite could only shake his head and produce his one word of English…"difficult".
No matter, we thanked him and drove on to Avlonari proper and found that the village was terraced steeply into the hillside, sleepy in the Sunday sunshine. We parked and walked the winding narrow roads up and up with just the occasional cat to peer at us. We saw one or two old ladies clad in regulation black wool dress, cardigan, and thick stockings, black head scarves pulled tight round their nut brown, weathered faces. Did they all have bow legs or was it just the effect of the black stockings?
They looked at us with mild interest, early yet for tourists, and then looked away. Suddenly a different old lady appeared, banging open her door to shake a blue mat which she threw down on to the road and started to sweep with vigorous strokes. She was dressed from head to toe in every colour of the rainbow, the pattern of her jumper completely different from that of her skirt. Even her stockings were multi coloured. Her head was bare. She raised her broom in salute, a broad smile revealing one tooth in the middle of her upper jaw. We smiled and waved, I longed to photograph her silhouetted against her white house with scarlet Geraniums and butter-golden Freesias in pots on her windowsills but didn't quite dare ask.
Whatever did her black clad neighbours think of her? Did they like her, perhaps envy her eccentricity or did they talk about her behind her back? She didn't look as if she would care much either way. We carried on up past cacti, purple Bougainvillea and sprays of yellow, rather like our Winter Jasmine but much more exuberant. The Oleanders weren't in flower though they lined the streets and balconies and would be wonderful in the summer, but the Freesias were beautiful, heavy headed and strongly perfumed gold or lilac, wafting their perfume so that we could tell where they were before seeing them.
We reached the top and a large church in a big open courtyard bounded by white walls. Perfect for football and there in the far corner, kicking a ball back and forth, bouncing it noisily off the walls was a small band of boys, about eight to ten years old. One came over to us with a lurching, stumbling walk. He dribbled and drooled, laughing at nothing and following us as we walked and took photographs of the distant mountains and the sea. He pulled at my dress and butted us gently with his head like a small mountain goat. We walked towards the other boys and spotting him with us they called to him, instantly vigilant, instantly protective, not wanting him to be a nuisance, but for his sake, not ours.
He joined them immediately with just a small backward glance at us and they all moved off down the winding street. How safe he seemed up here. Everyone would know him; know which

house he belonged to and who to return him to if he wandered too far. He could move quite freely and come to no harm. I couldn't quite imagine the same freedom in England.

The Lombard Tower was tall against the sky behind the church but both it and the church were locked and so we set off back down the streets to the car and on the way noticed a small taverna which looked open. We ordered coffee. Unfortunately the immediate Greek response to this order seems to be the eager offer of Nescafe or 'Nes'. They seem to feel that all foreigners will regard this as a great treat, as it may well be to many, but not to me. No good asking for filter coffee or black coffee; they shrug, they look disappointed, eventually they offer Turkish coffee which is too strong even for my palate and has a strange, grainy consistency.
We persevered, I had Greek coffee and a glass of water, John had Ouzo and iced coffee, also strong and plain. We sat on the narrow veranda and John sketched a doorway opposite, while the world gradually passed us by. Actually, hardly anybody passed us by, the ubiquitous hair-gelled youths on small motorbikes, some alone, some in pairs, the one on the back with his hands in his pockets to demonstrate to any stray female that he is no sissy who needs to hold on, one or two old men in pickup trucks, no-one else at all. Tremendous trilling bird song soared up from the cages fixed to the outside wall opposite in the sunshine. The cages were none too big and all the towns seem to have them strung outside, filling the air with their sweet racket. Would the birds sing like that if they weren't happy? Perhaps they are not singing, perhaps they are crying…calling for help to the free birds they see flying above them. No good to think about it too much. Unalterable.

John finished his Ouzo and his sketch and we paid and sauntered back to the car.
We left the rainbow lady, the laughing boy and the singing birds to their Sunday.

When I visited 'The Dragon Hall', a very old merchant's house in King Street in Norwich, I loved the story of how the archaeologists had uncovered a beautiful, small carving of a dragon which had been hidden for centuries under plaster in the roof space and when 'discovered' was as bright and beautiful as the day it was carved.
It was a lovely parallel to my allowing some of my layers to be peeled away on a very testing bit of learning I was doing at the time. Lynn

# THE DRAGON

The dragon
Hidden in the roof
Protected,
We don't know she's there.
Colours rich, teeth,
Coil of tail, humped, ready to spring,
Centuries on her back.

Hands, careful, lovingly
Lifting gently the layers that protect her.
Exposing with expertise.

They know what they are doing.

Sleeping dragon wakes,
Stretches, yawns, sniffs the air
Scales alive with colour
And opens an eye on the modern world.

John and I stayed overnight in Canterbury en route for our first holiday together in France quite a short time after we had started 'going out'. The strangeness and uncertainty of starting a new relationship after 25 years with my previous husband were very evident at that time. Lindsay

## A Bath in Canterbury

I decided that a long soak in the bath would be blissful and, gathering up my bits and pieces, I headed for the bathroom.

"Good idea", John smiled up at me. "I might join you in a minute."

Oh. This stopped me in my tracks somewhat. I supposed, thinking about it, that this was what one did on a first night away together in a hotel, en route for France. I couldn't very well just run a bath, get out a metaphorical loofah and set to. This was supposed to be the stuff of romance. A little porcelain bowl held those rather mean sachets of bubble bath and shampoo and I emptied a couple of them into the water which frothed up obligingly. I wished that I had (a) no cellulite and (b) larger bosoms. However, I was still in my pre-settling down skinny state and the light from the strip bulb over the sink was flattering; could be worse.

This was not being pathetically sexist. I bet that you could challenge the most hardened feminist, the most liberated intellectual and they would still have to admit to peering backwards into the mirror at their thighs and wishing that they had the smooth, tanned limbs of the model girls in the papers and magazines who taunt us from the pages every day. Anyhow, I think they are airbrushed out, whatever that means.

I got into the bath, sank down into the silky water and relaxed. I am not an energetic washer. I prefer to soak slowly and gently, taking my time. Every now and then I peered through into the bedroom where John was still engrossed with his book. I didn't quite know what to expect. Would he come through and start washing my back, gradually 'losing the soap' and having to hunt for it in exciting and unlikely places? Would he simply climb in with me? I checked the dimensions of the bath. I would have to let some of the water out if he did. I closed my eyes and waited to see what would happen.

Just as I was drifting off into a doze I became aware that he had come through into the bathroom and had crouched down by the bath. This was it. I opened my eyes to see if he had any clothes on.

"This is very interesting". He held a large, glossy-paged book that he had been reading on the bed. "Monet was a collector of Japanese prints. Look at these, aren't they lovely"?

I looked and as he explained and pointed out the different aspects of each picture and tiny little details that I wouldn't immediately have seen, I became interested and forgot that I was naked in a bath in Canterbury.

"There's a collection of his prints at his house in Giverny, shall we go there"?

Of course, it sounded wonderful and I told him so. He seemed to have lost track of the conversation a bit and wandered back to lie on the bed. He had spread out maps of France and was busily sorting out a route that could happily encompass Giverny.

So, that was it! No need to panic. This was what happened when you lounged in a bath with a relatively strange man in the adjoining room.

He would talk to you about the thrill of Japanese art!

I cycle home from Lindsay's in the dark and pass the huge 'muck heap' on a sharp bend-I often think I'll overshoot the corner! In my imagining, Mellors is a strapping Norfolk lad-curly hair, a ready smile, big hands and full of vigour! (From about the early fifties). Lynn

## Mellors of the Muck Heap.

I'm Mellors of the muck heap
I am a handsome chap.
The village girls all love me and sit upon my lap!
I have a secret place I go-
End of Dinah's Lane
Between the A11 and the Peterborough train.

It's here the farmer piles his muck
From horses, cows and sheep
But it's where I have a little fun
And then a little sleep.

The girls don't care about the stink
They wait in yonder hollow
I give them all a little wink
And bid them all to follow.

I'm Mellors of the muck heap
I live in Spooner Row
I am a happy farmer's lad
But there's something you should know

You can choose to meet me-
But if you go for 'It'
Like lots of girls before you
You'll end up in the ----------doghouse

Now you may chide and you may say
"Enough of your philanderin' "
Them girls don't know what
they got comin'
When my hands start meanderin!

But I know they like my little games
It always makes'em smile
And I'm still the King of the Castle
Atop my smelly pile!!

With five hours to kill in Dublin Airport waiting for a transfer flight, I had armed myself with newspaper, novel, large cappuccino and an extra large Danish pastry. All was well with the world. I curled up in a brown leather armchair novel in one hand, pastry in the other and prepared to enjoy my enforced 'time out'.
I had not however been prepared for the amazingly piercing sound of metal on tiles... Jo

## MEZZANINE CHAIRS - DUBLIN AIRPORT.

Saturday morning,
Travelling alone
Piercing noises surround;
The mezzanine Tannoy babbles
and drones
And screeching chairs abound.

Curled up in an armchair,
Watching the world
As it sips and chatters and texts;
Shrieking chairs scour the squares
Of the grey tiled mezzanine floor.

Sport on the big screen,
With sub-titled news
Flickers then stops, then moves on;
But the squealing of chairs like
nails down a board,
Will continue long after I'm gone.

We all decided that we wanted to go away for a weekend together. No work, no men just the three of us with the opportunity to read, write, take photographs, sketch , drink wine and talk and talk and talk and that is exactly what we did.

We found a little cottage called Seaforth in Aldeburgh, in Suffolk, right by the sea and a minute from the pub - what could be better. We had a great weekend, exactly what we wanted and so often in life the things you plan don't turn out as you wish.

We decided to set ourselves the task of writing a piece about Seaforth within a time limit and the end results were exactly in the spirit of the weekend.

We sent them to the charming lady who rented out Seaforth at the time and she was so pleased! She said that her children and grandchildren all loved the cottage and loved to write and paint and had spent their childhood holidays there over the years.

Alas, it is now sold. Time moves on and we'll go back to Aldeburgh but not to Seaforth

*Written by Lynn on a very silly weekend in Seaforth cottage, Aldeburgh, when we all decided to speculate about how it got its name! Absolutely must be read with Suffolk (or, failing that, Norfolk) accent.*

**SEAFORTH .... Lynn**

**The Silly Tale of Seaforth Cottage.**

**Young Maddy Plowright fell in love**
**Lock, stock and smoking barrel.**
**She loved his face and his bonny hair**
**And his handsome sailor's apparel.**

**"Hello", he said, "Young pretty maid**
**Do you come here often?**
**I'm Able Seaman Seaforth**
**And I come from down at Slaughden!"**

**He, in turn, admired her too,**
**Her curls and her neat figure**
**Her ruby lips and eyes of blue**
**All bonny Aldeburgh vigour!**

**Well! These young loves**
**At highest tide**
**On a starry, starry, night,**
**Wandered down the shingly bank**
**To where the foam was bright.**

**(A jealous man her father was**
**He watched as their love grew**
**Mad as a box of frogs he was**
**But no one really knew!!!)**

**"I love you Maddy!**
**I love you dear! Make me a serious vow!**
**As I'm off to sea and I need your troth**
**Let's seal our love right now!!!"**

**So, just as they were about to get**
**To that place above all others**
**Her father from the darkness lurched**
**And shot the star crossed lovers!!!**

**"No Jolly Tar will have my girl!"**
**He bellowed to the waves.**
**"Nor any man, nor any boy**
**Nor any blackguard knaves!!!**

**Now Maddy's broken hearted Ma**
**Looked on from the cottage doorway**
**So upset was she by what had passed**
**She sailed away to Norway!**

**The townsfolk named the empty house**
**For Seaforth and his bride**
**And the gun and the shingle**
**And the starry, starry night**
**And the very, very, very high tide.**

**THE END!**

## Seaforth - Lindsay

Alex and I used to go to Seaforth every year – towards the end of the long school holidays, and sometimes in between. We were very important on our last journey there, important because despite our ages, twelve and nine respectively, we were allowed to travel alone. We always travelled by coach. We each had a box with a clip top lid which contained sandwiches in grease proof paper and a chocolate biscuit, a Penguin or a Tunnocks Caramel Wafer. My favourite sandwich was fish paste and Alex liked egg which was rather awkward sometimes because when he unclipped the lid on the coach, hours after Mum had made the sandwiches there was usually a rather terrible eggy smell so that he had to do a lot of prominent commenting on how delicious his egg sandwiches were and a lot of lip smacking and chomping just so people understood. I suppose that what with Alex's eggs and my fish paste we can't have been very pleasing travelling companions but people didn't seem to mind.

When we arrived at Aldeburgh Auntie Phyllis would meet us and we'd walk along the sea front to the cottage, chattering away and telling her all our news - showing her new scars on knees and Alex's latest boil. (He always had at least one boil on his neck, goodness knows why, he must have been quite well nourished what with all those eggs) but still he didn't seem to mind. He was quite known for them at school, there'd often be an admiring little crowd round him in the play ground exclaiming at the gleaming ferocity of his latest eruption.

Auntie Phyllis would listen and tut and say, "Well I never" as if she really meant it and soon we'd be at the cottage and tumbling in through the front door to make sure that all was as we last left it. We always checked the photos by the door, pictures of the cottage decorated for Carnival time, pictures of Alex and me holding crabs aloft in the little front garden and then we'd check out the puzzles and games in the little chest of drawers. Woe betide Auntie Phyllis if anything had changed!

In the evenings we would tune in the big radio-big as a cupboard, it stood on the floor in the corner and we'd sit in front of it with mugs of hot chocolate and Alex would twist the dials making it squeal and whistle until he got something reasonably clear. Auntie Phyllis would cover her ears and pretend that we had made her go deaf and we would shout to make her understand us and she'd pretend to  mishear and give funnier and funnier answers until we'd nearly burst ourselves laughing.

When Alex and I were thirteen and ten our parents took us abroad to live. Dad had a new job in Cologne which sounded very exciting but wasn't, and we went to an English speaking school which was ok I suppose but we missed England and the only contact we had with Auntie Phyllis was by postcard. We didn't return to England for nearly  six years and during that time Auntie Phyllis wrote to say that she had moved in to a small sheltered flat just outside Aldeburgh, a place with a warden because her knees were quite bad but she had kept Seaforth and was letting it. We felt betrayed and outraged because she was inextricably linked in our minds with Seaforth and what would become of the big radio and what would strangers think of our photographs by the door? How dare they be allowed to look in to our lives and wonder about us?

When we got back to England, Alex suggested that we get the coach, just the two of us, like the old days and go to visit Auntie Phyllis and to see Seaforth so we could tell her about it, the garden and so on because she didn't go there any more, she had it looked after by some sort of agency. We got off the coach and it felt wrong because Auntie Phyllis wasn't there to meet us but we didn't say this to each other.

We reached Seaforth but just as we crossed over from the sea wall a car pulled up in the little square and a family spilled out, small children with coloured shrimping nets and a stupid, jolly looking father with baggy shorts and a stripy tee shirt and they ran up the little path to Seaforth. The door was flung open by a young woman in jeans. Jeans! She swept them all inside, shrieking and laughing and they banged the door shut.

Alex and I didn't speak; we turned and walked away in the direction of the sheltered flats where Auntie Phyllis waited for us in her new, secure world of alarm cords, grab rails and wardens.

Safely away from the tang of the
seaweed and the scream of the gulls,
she waited for death.

## SEAFORTH - Jo

The lobster pots lay in disarray against the wall, wisps of seaweed entangled in the twine. It made her think of the wet tendrils of his hair when he emerged from the tin bath set before the fire, tousled and dark.

He had always kept his hair long, even when they had known each other as children playing amongst the nets and debris that surrounded the fishing boats pulled up on the shingle beach. When they had argued she used to pull his hair but he would just laugh at her and pull away, dashing across the pebbled beach daring her to follow him; she had no chance of catching him, but she ran anyway.

It had been a carefree existence and they had grown up like brother and sister. As long as she could remember they had roamed the beach; free to come and go as they pleased, leaving their fathers to the fishing and their mothers to the constant worry for their men's safe return.

Storms always brought the tight knit community even closer together, with the women's shared fears for their men's safety but to the children storms meant excitement and a beach to explore the following morning. Driftwood, bottles, ropes and unusual seaweeds were strewn as far as the eye could see; an Aladdin's cave waiting to be discovered.

As time went by he began to spend more time around the men. Some days he would go to sea with his father leaving her on the shore, putting off the time when she would have to return home and help her mother. Collecting driftwood for the fire had been a childhood task she had enjoyed, but now she was older she was expected to help with the washing, the baking and the scrubbing of the floors as well.

A task she did enjoy was filling the tin bath. After she had dragged it from its resting place in the outhouse and placed it in front of the fire, she filled it with hot water from the kettle and large black pans, so that it was ready for her father to step into when he returned from a night's fishing. It seemed to her a great pleasure to be responsible for changing the cold, fish smelling, spray soaked fisherman into a warm, red cheeked, soap scented father who would take her on his knee and tell her stories of giant squid and mermaids fair.

As summer passed, the childhood friends grew to teenagers and their boisterous friendship became shy courtship.
He had become a fisherman like his father and grandfather before him and she began to recognise the same fear her mother must have felt every time her father had pushed his boat at eventide into the heaving waves.
They married in the autumn and moved into Seaforth, a tiny fisherman's cottage, a few streets away from her childhood home. The childhood friends had become soul mates and life was good.

But today was different.
Today no boat had come ashore in the early dawn. It was not the first time a fishing boat had been late returning home but this time it was his. She gazed again at the lobster pots stacked up against the wall. Again the vision of his dark, tousled hair came into her mind. But this time she thought she saw it billowing in the waves, trapped under an upturned boat; she turned away and went inside to get her coat; fastening it against the dawn's chill she went back out and ran down to the beach. The shingle crunched under her feet and gazing out to sea she made her way to the water's edge. Long hours she waited in vain until persuaded by a stoical but compassionate mother she eventually returned to Seaforth. She stoked the fire and heated the water, laid the tin bath on the floor and waited.
Dusk drew in and still she waited. Memories of that long ago beach flew into her mind and again her child self was chasing him across the pebbles, his hair flying in the breeze. In her mind's eye he turned and looked at her, brown eyes laughing. Her heart ached for him. Slowly she filled the bath with the steaming water, fighting back her tears.

A lantern, a footstep on the path; they had come with news. She moved towards the door with faltering steps, dread weighing heavy on her aching heart. The door opened. Hair dark and tousled, brown eyes tired but brimming with a love that enveloped her, he stepped towards her, arms outstretched. She moved towards him and as they clung together in an embrace that excluded the world, she whispered a silent "thank you" to the sea.

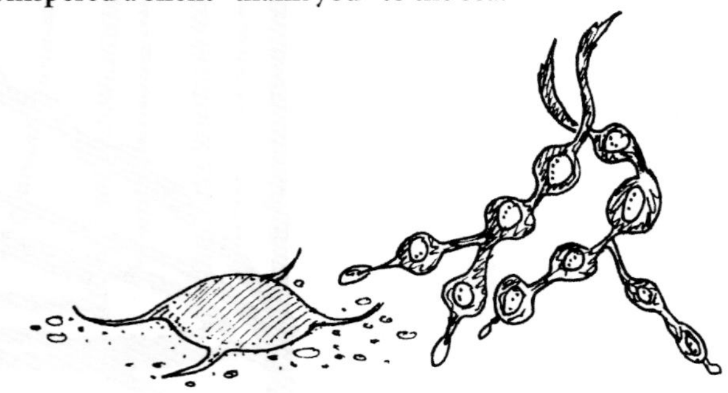

*Written after a very hot summer day with my parents - watching and listening to a skylark from the top of Overstrand cliffs. Lynn*

## TODAY

Today I saw a skylark
It dipped and weaved
In a fragile bubble of sound
Which wavered
Across the cliff top grass.

Like a tiny paper shape,
Lost in a painted sky,
Flipped this way and that
On warm breeze
Chasing its own song.

*This is about my dear Dad and his struggle at the end of his life and how I always think of him when I hear Skylarks singing and how he's free from pain now. It's also about dying, in the in between stage when someone has first gone. Lynn*

## LETTING GO

Bubbling brook of sound
The skylark rises
Sweet waves of untrapped pleasure
The exquisite essence of summer
Of the struggle to ascend.
Small
Perfect
Free
I can almost catch it.

I think of your bird spirit
Struggling to go on,
I hear you in that song
A tiny sound
And far beyond my noisy world.
Small
Perfect
Free
But I can't quite see you.

Life, bird, man,
Beating the breeze beneath.
Up, up through the blue.
Invisible,
Then my eyes locate you
Nearly hidden in the speckled atoms of this summer sky,
The sun behind dazzles
Until you disappear from sight
And I let you go.

*I wrote Jan's story years ago and I don't remember why. It's rather long and old fashioned now but Lynn and Jo like it and said 'put it in'. So I did! Lindsay*

Jan was annoyed. She marched resolutely down the path from her mother's front door, clicked the gate, a little too firmly behind her and set off for the bus stop. Her heels clacked along the pavement and as she walked she muttered to herself; little agitated outbursts, exclaiming under her breath. She turned the corner and, failing to look properly before crossing the road, had to step back suddenly to avoid a motorcyclist and slipped off the kerb, twisting her ankle painfully in the process.
"Damn, damn", now she wasn't just annoyed, she was angry, angry with her mother and angry with herself. She stooped down to rub her ankle and saw that she had scuffed a bald patch on the heel of one of her new shoes; they had been an expensive bargain in the sales. She could hear her mother's voice in her head,
"It's not a bargain if you don't really need it".
Well, she wouldn't be discussing anything with her mother from now on, no more confiding, no more seeking advice, after all she wasn't a child anymore, time to grow up and keep her own counsel. She set off again and arrived at the bus stop just in time to see the bus, uncharacteristically on time for once, pulling out and sheer exasperation defeated her and stopped her from trying to flag it down. She flopped down on to the seat inside the bus shelter and leant back with a sigh.

The sun shone on her face and she tilted her head back to receive its comforting warmth. She would sit there until another bus or a taxi appeared and she would take whichever came first. Stretching her legs out in front of her to ease her ankle, which was beginning to throb, she allowed her mind to drift back over the problems that she had unwisely tried to discuss with her mother.
The main trouble was Nigel, her husband. She very much feared that the increasing distance and petty hostilities which had begun to creep in to their relationship might continue to grow, mainly because although she hardly wanted to admit it, even to herself, Nigel was mean, not just mean but narrow. He was not a man who had grown or expanded within his marriage, it was more as if he was increasingly defending his corner.
Then there was Jerry. Lord, what was she going to do about Jerry? She blushed at the thought that she had even considered discussing him with Mum. She must have been mad. The trouble was that every now and then, in amongst the 78 year old, hide bound jumble of her mother's mind would flash a spark of clear, even modern insight which caught you off balance and tricked you in to saying more than you had intended. Well, not any more she resolved and opening her eyes she looked to see if there was any sign of a bus. There was not and she closed her eyes again and resumed her pondering. It would have been okay if they hadn't had that stupid row on the Friday night…over nothing at all really, as these things often are.

Jan had got in to the habit of going out with her friend Carol twice a week, nothing fancy, a local cinema to laugh themselves sick at some daft new film or a drink at the pub, it made a change and they both looked forward to it. This particular Friday Nigel had seemed especially difficult, constantly delaying her and finding fault, finally he had vented his spleen by delivering a spiteful imitation of her voice on the phone to Carol.
"Hi Carol, meet you at Charlie's, don't be late darling!"
He pursed his lips and raised his shoulders in an effort to look feminine, his voice high, nasal and spiteful. God she thought, looking at him, God if you knew what you look like doing that!
"What's the problem Nigel? You know we go out for a drink and a gossip on Fridays. Why is that suddenly a problem?
"A drink, a gossip". He spat the words in his rage. "A chance to get half cut and see what you can pick up more like".
He surely couldn't think that. Didn't he know anything about her at all? Didn't he realise that the last thing she and Carol wanted on their nights out was to involve men. Men were a distraction, they would try to take over the conversation, subtly patronise the women and spoil the fun. If that was what Nigel thought then he was a fool. "You're jealous; you're mean, petty and jealous!"
And that was it. They descended in to the kind of damaging, destructive shouting that can't be retrieved once it's started. It had scared her. The violence of her feelings had made her shake and, grabbing her bag from the hall table she had fled.

She was too early for Carol and in no state to socialise and, catching sight of a taxi, probably headed back to the station she had hailed it and gone to Max's, a wine bar much used by local women. It was cleverly run by Max, not interested in women himself but sufficiently in tune with their feelings to provide exactly the right combination of casual chic, good wines and softly lit comfort. Men used Max's as well, it wasn't a problem but they instinctively knew that this was a place where the women were there in their own right and they expected to chat, read the paper or simply sit and drink without it meaning they were seeking company.
Jan picked the Times out of the stand by the coat pegs by the door, got herself a pale glass of cool white wine and headed for a corner table. She sat, gradually feeling the tension ease a little, sipping at her wine and occasionally pushing back the heavy drape of auburn hair which flopped forward over her face. She wasn't really reading the paper, her eyes scanned the words, her fingers turned the pages but very little of the content penetrated her brain which was still remorselessly playing with the words which had suddenly exploded from both of them with such unexpected force.
She stooped to pick up her bag from the floor and knocked against the table, rattling her glass so that it fell, spewing wine over the paper. It ran down on to her dress. She jumped up looking around for something to mop the table with. So engrossed had she been in her own thoughts that she hadn't noticed the young man sitting in the corner diagonally opposite, partially obscured by a pot plant (Max was having

a jungle period). He came over to her table holding out a bundle of paper napkins.
"Thanks, God I'm clumsy!" she was so anxious to clear up the mess that she took the napkins without really taking in where they were coming from but glancing up she noticed that the man was young, nice looking but definitely young and could therefore have no designs on her; just being helpful. She smiled and he ordered another glass of wine and asked her to join him.

Easing herself on the hard bus shelter bench and raising her face further in to the sun she smiled slightly at the memory of that first meeting. She honestly couldn't remember really how it had evolved from there, it just had; relatively harmless at first, or so she had kidded herself, using his age as a defence. This soon wore thin however. Younger than her he might have been but it was quite obvious that he found this older lady sophisticated, entertaining and very, very sexy. She seemed to him a much more attractive proposition that the generally rather vacant young women that he met at the odd party or club. It wasn't long before they fell joyously in to bed and Jan found that the last of her reservations about the age difference had vanished with Jerry's evident enthusiasm for her 39 year old body.
If Nigel suspected anything it wasn't apparent and her evening with Carol had drifted seamlessly into evenings with Jerry, causing her a lack of guilt which surprised her, when she troubled to think about it.

The problem was, she bent down to her now slightly swollen ankle...the problem was that Jerry was starting to become serious and she was becoming seriously tempted.
What to do? What to do?
Her mind had been churning lately in the circles which had led her to her mother's door. A chugging diesel engine and a blast of warm air heralded the arrival of a bus and, gathering up her bag, she got up, wincing a little as her weight bore down on to the ankle and climbed stiffly aboard.

Jan's mothers' name was Ellen. She had always rather liked it...a name of her generation which was now finding favour again, it was a solid name, capable but feminine and suited her well.
She dropped the net curtain back in place having watched Jan march down the garden path. She had tutted at the unnecessarily firm click of the gate and shaken her head slightly as she noted the clack-clack of the high heels on the pavement.
"She'll fall off those heels one of these fine days, stamping about like that!"
She had felt a mixture of exasperation and pity as she watched her child trying to march away from her troubles. Why did she come and confide such things? Ellen was 78 years old for Heavens' sake and these were private matters, not her business, not fit for her consideration, and yet she had always been pleased that Jan had talked to her so freely, shared her problems and her worries. People used to say,

"Those two, they're more like friends than mother and daughter".
She had smiled and shrugged but had been proud of it really. It takes work to build up a relationship like that; you don't just fall in to it. Well, she had worked at it and now look where it had got her! She had told Jan in no uncertain terms, "Your wedding vows are just that, vows, made for life-love honour and obey or whatever it was that they said nowadays." She had stuck to her vows, the ones that she had made all those years ago when she married Fred. She had stuck to them regardless and he had proved to be quite a selfish man, a bully really. Hard to forgive that in a man she thought with the detachment of hindsight.
She went through to the kitchen and put on the kettle. Her disagreement with Jan had shaken her up and she steadied herself with the familiar arrangement of the tea things on the old tray with the beaded edges. Vows were vows and that is how it should be. She had married Fred despite his failings, but then, she thought, suddenly sitting down on the kitchen chair, it was just as well that she had or there could have been hell and all to pay.
The kettle boiled, she got up and made the tea, putting it on the kitchen table and pouring a cup she sat back down. The steam rose up and misted her spectacles and she gazed through the warm haze, waiting for them to clear and thinking back over the years.
Yes, she had been glad to marry Fred; it had been the right thing to do. She had never been very happy at home; her parents relied too heavily on her. Her mother, a frail, whining lady, old before her years, and her father rather a lazy man.
"Just pop down to the shops for us will you Ellie? Get us a new loaf and perhaps you could knock up a few sandwiches. The lads from the darts club are coming tonight."
Ellie would trot about, obliging her father and answering her mother's querulous calls so that they could feel that they were in charge of the household without actually doing much.
It had been a bit difficult when Fred first came on the scene. She had found him very attractive in his soldier's uniform, home on leave, hair Bryllcreemed, slim and fit from his army training. He was a good dancer. Many was the night that they would dance straight through to the last waltz at the Moonlight Ballroom in Silver Street and still have the energy to cuddle up in the doorways on the way home. Actually, their 'cuddling up' had become rather more than that lately and Ellen knew that she and Fred were a proper couple. She also knew that there were some traits of Fred's character that she didn't much care for, but she supposed that all men were rather like that and he would probably change once they were married.
When he was going on his last tour of duty before being demobbed she went to see him off, standing on the platform waving a forlorn hand and feeling like the heroine in one of those sad black and white films of that era. She had watched until the train vanished, fighting down the flickerings of a

feeling of relief, and decided to pop in to the station buffet for a reviving cup of tea and a chat. The customers were mostly men, workers and men in the forces but it didn't matter. Ellen sometimes helped out in the station buffet, doing her bit for the war effort and she knew the ladies behind the counter quite well. Meg was on duty today. She liked Meg though she knew that she was a bit rough, what her mother would call 'common'. Meg could tell a joke like a man, better in fact. She would spin it out until she had wrung just enough out of it and then deliver the punch line with a whoop of laughter that made you laugh even if the joke didn't.

"Here," said Meg leaning over the counter dangerously close to a pile of sandwiches, her cleavage squashed on to the counter top, "have you heard the one about ...."She launched in to a long, rambling and none too clean joke in a sort of stage whisper which could easily have been heard on the other platform. The inevitable punch line came and Ellen had to laugh despite herself. It was a bit near the knuckle and she looked around embarrassed, to see if anyone had heard. She met the eye of a rather nice looking young soldier, nice looking but thin and pale with a flop of fair hair hanging over his forehead. Not the least bit like Fred. He grinned at her and Meg and shrugged and bringing his tea over to the counter ordered another cup and one for each of them. The three chatted and laughed together. She supposed, looking back, that she should have realised then the danger signals, but it seemed innocent enough. She was used to the easy camaraderie of the buffet and all the women who helped there did there bit to cheer up the lads.

They both headed in the same direction home and walked together from the station and arranged to meet the next day for a walk and ' a bit more of a chat'. Ellen had gone about her chores at home in a sort of dream. Fred seemed a long way off and her parents' usual demands made a backdrop to her thoughts. She could see herself working as a voluntary nurse in one of those big old houses that were commissioned in war time. You saw them on the films; the beautiful young deb. in flattering nurse's uniform wheeling the handsome but delicate young officer out in the grounds. He might have a leg in plaster or some sort of wound that wasn't too disfiguring! They would fall in love, of course. She could see it all. She started when her mother asked for a 'fill up' for her cup of tea, "Come on girl whatever are you thinking of?" Whatever indeed.

Fred's letters which she had eagerly awaited and pounced on almost before they hit the mat now became something of a nuisance. She answered them, naturally, but rather as if they were homework, a necessity to get over and done with, and she was guiltily aware of the change in her attitude as she sucked the top of her pen and struggled to find the words of affection that had filled pages so easily not long ago. She had gone beyond her initial friendship with James, a name which she infinitely preferred to Fred! By now they were lovers and she could not feel badly about anything which could bring her such joy.

Ellen pushed back the wooden chair, making a scraping noise on the tiled floor. The light was fading and the kitchen becoming dim. She took the tea tray to the sink and then, going to the corner cupboard took out a bottle of Bell's Whisky, poured a generous tot in to a tumbler and sat down again. She didn't put on the light; she didn't need light to see her memories. The first sip sent a stream of warmth melting down her throat and in to her stomach. She cradled the glass and looked back again over the years, her eyes filming slightly. James loved her in a way that she had not experienced with Fred. He cared about her feelings, listened to her conversation, weighed what she said and loved to talk and laugh and hold her. She had not known that there was such love as this and she had hoarded it like a miser hoarding gold against harder times.

Fred's letters had become more ardent. Perhaps he had noticed the subtle change in her replies and begun to wonder if something was up. Ellen was more attractive than she would ever realise, her sleek coppery hair and hourglass figure were combined with a fresh faced innocence, rather like a child grown too big, which mad and irresistible combination more than one man had noticed in the past but Ellen had never noticed them, Fred took care of that. He wrote suggesting that they speed things up and get married on his next leave. In fact, he added, he had already applied for the special licence, a move which had so incensed Ellen that he had nearly stymied himself altogether.

James too was growing more serious. He wanted her to quit her home. He could see that she was taken advantage of, and resented it for her. He knew of Fred but discounted him out of hand. "Come up North with me" he had said when she last met him. His family had a business up there and his elderly father was only waiting for James' demob. so that he could retire and take a back seat at last. She had loved him utterly and never loved like that again.

Ellen looked down at the empty glass…she didn't remember drinking it. She poured another tot, smaller this time and added some water to it.

Just as James and Fred were stepping up the pressure several things happened at once. Her mother had a stroke which appeared to reduce her father to a far worse state of helplessness than it did her mother, and Ellen suddenly realised why she had been feeling so tired and dreary and why the task of feeding softly scrambled egg in to the lopsided and drooling mouth of her mother had several times resulted in waves of nausea, making her fly to the bathroom to sweat and retch over the toilet. She was pregnant! The age-old joker had popped up like the music hall Punch, "There you go little girl, you've had your fun, now you must pay!" She could remember to this day staring at herself in the bathroom mirror with the shock of discovery staring back at her.

She talked to James and surprised herself with her implacable calm in the face of his pleading. She could not go away with him 'up North', abandoning her parents just when they needed her most. She had married Fred as soon as he returned, which fortunately was very soon after her discovery.
Yes, Ellen sat on, in the darkening kitchen, she had married Fred and nursed her parents and sent her love away. What else was there for her to do? She had honoured her wedding vows for twenty five long years. After the twenty five years, Fred didn't die. He left her! Said he had fallen in love with Marjorie Roberts who did the bar at the British Legion, and after the first shock and anger she had to confess to an overwhelming feeling of gratitude at her release.

She got up and snapped on the light. So, Jan had got a man…a young one at that, apparently. She had never much cared for her son in law, mealy-mouthed, mean spirited sort of a chap. A younger man would be hard to keep but Jan might get a year of love and passion, perhaps two, or even ten, who could tell? Real love not the apologetic, lip-serving, routine love of a lifetime's adherence to a set of marriage vows.

She went out to the hall. The trouble with getting old was that you forgot people's phone numbers, even your own daughter's. She looked through the pad on the small table. Here it was…Jan. She put one bony finger in the dial and smiled as the phone started to ring.

*Years ago, whilst at college, I came across an image of a woman in a fur coat. There was something lonely and mysterious about her.*
*I changed the image into a small screen print of a lone figure, hair blowing in a cold wind, placing her at the end of an alleyway, lit by a single street lamp. I often wondered what her story was and why I had placed her there on her own.*
*This is the beginning of her story. Jo*

## FRENCH STORY

The long fur coat, with its collar turned up against the icy winter chill, kept her warm as she walked quickly through the dimly lit streets of Paris.

Autumn seemed a long time ago now.
The trees had changed swiftly from their summer green to wearing mantles of ochre, burnt umber and crimson.
It had been a warm autumn and the lowering sun had illuminated the trees as if they had been tinged with gold leaf.
As the leaves fell they had created a russet carpet in the parks and avenues.
Strolling couples had walked hand in hand wrapped in each others eyes. Small children had thrown gleeful handfuls of leaves up into the blue sky to watch them tumble and float around them finally settling again on the paths and lawns.
Across the boating lake in the middle of the park leaves scudded like tiny boats, buffeted and blown by the warm autumn breeze.

Now as she passed the small lake, the waters were frozen and the leaves were captured in a crystallized patchwork of browns, blacks and greys.
Whilst she had been walking past the shop fronts and the cafés the dim lighting had seemed friendly but now amongst the trees of the park the lamplight seemed to cast shadows more threatening than comforting.
With her head down and collar held tightly against the icy wind she followed the path across to the edge of the park.
The shadow fingers that had seemed to reach for her, released her from their grasp as she stepped through the small iron gateway and out onto the pavement.

The lights of a nearby café beckoned and she made her way across the cobbled street. The uneven surface was familiar beneath her feet and her boots made a gentle clicking sound as she approached the doorway of the café.
No-one else was out on that bitter night and as she glanced down the street all that could be seen was the newly forming frost glistening on the cobbles.
She pushed the long brass handle of the café door and felt a rush of warm air burst through the widening gap, only to cool immediately as it hit the wall of ice cold air outside.

Inside, the bright lights reflected from the mirrored walls which gave the room the appearance of being much larger than it really was. Sounds of a singer crooning in a back room drifted towards her as she made her way towards a small table in the corner near the window.

Undoing her coat she sat down and looked across at the counter. A waiter in a crisp white shirt and black trousers came over to her, a long white apron around his waist and a note pad in his hand. She ordered coffee and a pastry, sat back in her chair and began to take in the scene around her.
Only three other people were in the room, an old man reading a newspaper and two younger men playing cards, glasses of Pernod and a jug of water on the table in front of them. They had taken no notice as she came in and still gave no sign that they were aware of her presence. The waiter brought her coffee and the pastry and returned to his duties behind the counter, wiping and replenishing the silver coffee machine.

As she sipped her coffee, its warmth flowed through her and she removed her coat, hanging it over an empty chair. The pastry was sweet and sticky and reminded her of times when, as a child, she and a friend had tried to eat a whole pastry without licking the sugar flakes from their lips; they had never succeeded, although they had tried many times!

The old man folded his newspaper, paid his bill at the counter and left, letting in a chill draught as he opened the heavy glass door.
Her coffee and pastry were finished, but there was still time remaining before she needed to set off for the meeting place. She signalled the waiter and ordered another coffee. As she waited for it to arrive, her mind drifted back to the last time that she had sat alone waiting for a coffee; it had been at the end of the summer and she had sat at a table amongst the trees on the boulevard, never guessing how her life was about to change.

The waiter placed the coffee in front of her and she jolted back to the present, smiling her thanks to him. Gazing through the plate glass of the café's front window she could see the first flakes of snow beginning to drift down from the sky. She watched their stately passage down to the cobbles where they lay amongst the sparkling frost but the chill wind blew the snow cloud away and it stopped releasing its flakes, moving away to where warmer air would allow them to fall in billowing clouds. For now the air was too cold and only the sparkling frost was allowed to rest like sprinkled sugar in the alleys and streets of Paris.

The second coffee was finished and it was time to leave. She lifted her coat from the chair and drew it around her, turning up the collar and fastening the belt against the cold to come. She walked over to the counter and asked how much she owed, once she had paid, she made her way to the door and left the café. Even though she was wrapped up against the cold and the fur lining of her boots was warm, she could still feel the icy fingers of the frosty night against her face. Turning down a side street lit by dull gas lamps she looked around her. Still no-one else had ventured out into the bitter cold and she was alone; her shadow cast itself ahead of her and then receded as she neared the next lamp.

(A loud report in the next street made her heart miss a beat; the cold, sharp crack of a single shot. She halted in her tracks, her heart pounding in her ears. She could not give up now, the decision had been made.)

It was not far to the meeting place now and yet she could hardly believe that it was at last going to take place. The frozen cobbles were slippery in places and she had to tread carefully. At the end of the street she could see the sign showing that the small alley to the left was a dead end. So close now, so very close. This was the way it was meant to be.
Dark, cold, crisp and silent.
She had known for a long time that this was the way that it would happen and she felt content.
Some things could only have one outcome.

People can make choices and take directions but sometimes it is better to stop and not fight against the inevitable flow. This was the decision she had taken; not to fight, not any more, it only caused heartache and regret.

And so, here she was; no bag, no belongings, only what she was wearing.
This was the only way. Take nothing that would cause suspicion, nothing that would give away her intention; nothing but a young woman walking through the streets of Paris.
No-one would guess and no-one would remember.

*The following is a 'Parisian snapshot in time' taken from a trip to France with my 'new man' (now my husband).*
*Lindsay*

## The Patron

We walked back through the streets-fortunately John has a good sense of direction and pretty soon we were pushing open the glass door into the restaurant which was still brightly lit and obviously still serving. Several tables were full, mainly with French who nearly all seemed to be simultaneously smoking, eating and talking non-stop. We found a table next to a window which opened on to the street and placed our order with the waiter who came over quite speedily. I suppose he was keen to get to the end of his day but he was still pleasant in an efficient, no time to waste sort of way. While we ate and talked and drank our wine, the other tables gradually began to empty. As each set of people got up to go, the patron came smoothly forward and produced the ladies' coats; he seemed to know which was which without being told. He had a word for each of them, giving the impression, flatteringly, that they were all valuable acquaintances, all beautiful, fragile creatures who couldn't possibly be expected to put on their own coats.

Once he had soothed and smoothed them out of the door, he went over to a table to one side and sat with his back to the wall, beneath a huge gilt-framed mirror which reflected the sparkling glasses and bottles behind the bar. He tucked a large, stiff white napkin into his collar and spread it carefully over his immaculate shirt front. He poured a glass of pale white wine from a large carafe which had been set in front of him as he sat down and he waited. I say waited, but he didn't wait long! The door swung open and a man I had noticed earlier at a fish stall located under the bright awning of the restaurant came in bearing a platter piled with cracked ice, wedges of lemon and seafood of every description; Prawns, langoustines, a whole lobster and little dobs of caviar. He set this dish in front of the patron who received it graciously with a slight nod of the head and a faint smile. The man was dismissed and vanished back out of the door. Adjusting his napkin-you could almost see his juices beginning to work - he raised his glass in our direction and gestured to the plate in front of him.

"Would you care to have some?"

His gesture and his raised eyebrows asked this question.

We smiled and toasted him with our glasses.

"Thank you, no" said our look.

Heaven knows what he would have done if we had said, "Yes please" and gleefully joined him at his table, helping ourselves to prawns and raiding his basket of bread rolls. None the less, it was a pleasant gesture and, having made it, he set to with a will, cracking the lobster claws loudly and efficiently and making great inroads in to his wine.

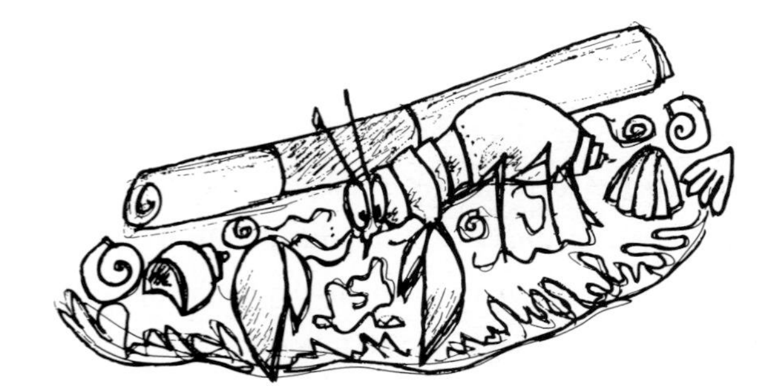

After serious consideration by the members of CUSP, :Lindsay, Lynn and Jo, in one of the planning meetings held in the Agricultural Bar of the Boars at Spooner Row felt that they would allow a small section for the husbands, John D, John R and Philip.

**Lindsay's husband, John wrote this poem while they holidayed on the Greek island of Euboea:**

**At the furthest point of Euboea, 'Isle of Kine'**
**From where Kimi's ferries sail to Skyros,**
**Tilted planes of shale, grey, ochreous, sandy**
**And rusty strata in waves and whorls**
**Lap out into the clear Aegean Sea.**

**And did Homer's feet tread here, or**
**Dip like these into the cool calm water,**
**And seeing, did he colour words**
**To tell the fates of Greeks, of**
**Boys and girls becoming almost gods,**
**In lines of slanted ochre, grey and**
**Sandy stone, lapping out,**
**Slipping into salt sea,**
**Out towards Skyros and beyond to Troy?**

**March 2001**

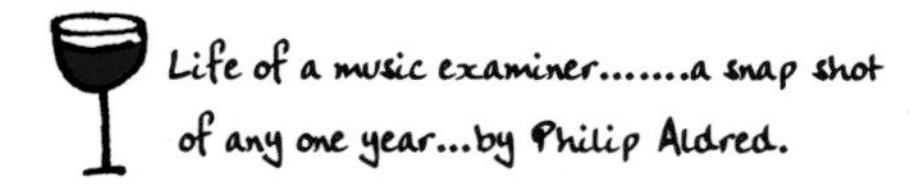


Music examining has taken me to many places: Sri Lanka, Indonesia, Thailand, Hong Kong, Borneo, Malaysia, Singapore, Canada, Malta, Greece, Wales, Scotland, Eire, Northern Ireland and England.

So many different, exciting, diverse landscapes, seas, cities, towns, villages, religions, cultures, food, people and languages, but all with one thing in common…music; the love of it and the desire to perform, always shining brightly.

Exams covering all instruments - including Piano, Keyboard, Woodwind, Brass, Strings, Drum Kit, Guitar, Organ, Voice, Music Theatre, Pop Vocals and Conducting.
Candidates arriving for their exams on elephants, water buffalo drawn carts, tuk-tuks, in cars, buses, taxis…on foot… each candidate unique, each exam a different experience.. special in so many different ways.
Ages from four to eighty two…abilities from beginner to internationally recognised 'stars' all are equal in the examination situation.
The young girl performing a piano exam with only a stump for a left arm…having been caught in a bomb blast…and playing so brilliantly!
Another young girl offering a 'bribe' of a 'sweetie' as she leaves the room only to close her hand tightly when I say, " I cannot accept bribes"... to which she replies, " Go on, have a sweetie, did I pass?" I answer, "All I can say is, enjoy the rest of your day and by the way I think your hand is very sticky now!"
A monkey enters the exam room in Kandy, Sri Lanka as a candidate performs a Pre - Prep examination…the monkey pops up on to the piano, looks around, the candidate carries on playing…I take my watch from the table and hide it as bright eyes focus on the shiny strap. Candidate passed… monkey got a Distinction!
A six foot candidate with the build of a prop forward, a huge presence in the room, there for a singing exam… opens his mouth to sing and an exquisite high counter tenor voice fills the room…not the sound you expect to hear from such a frame but, oh, was it worth listening to! Such a privilege.

All candidates are the same…all have so much to offer and the joy when they realise they have performed well is so tangible.

I am very lucky to do what I do.

Here's to the next tour!

*We are all re-homed, some of us by choice.......but all with love.*
*Kizzy, Lynn, Murphy and John.*

*A day in the life of......*

Soft breath in the morning, panting at bedside, ready for a new day.
Thundering down stairs, older frame cautious and careful at safer pace
Marshalled walk, stimulated by overnight smells and movement of wildlife large and small.
Galloping, bouncing and pouncing, strong noses searching grass tunnels, stopping to survey the fields ahead.
Through the year irritated by ice balled legs, soggy coats, seeds and tangles suffering necessary towelling and grooming.
Rolling in foul substances, washed out or dried
Attentive, uninterruptible waiting for breakfast toast crust tit bits (and a grape!)

Games in the garden, grandchildren caring, visitors challenged with deep throaty warnings. Friends welcomed with a bone or soft toy
Hide and seek, chasing toys, challenge and obedience.
Rakes, combs, brushes, scissors and clippers - groomed for comfort more than show.
Chorus of soft munching and crunching-the tinkle of collar on metal dish
Lying in doorways, conscious of movement.
Later, walks with road discipline, followed by instant relaxation, sleeping until supper.
Lengthy attempts at cross species communication, with patience, frustration and humour at our attempts to understand.
Deep dark eyes, smiling teeth, grasping and pushing paws in play
Vying for affection - giving in return
Pack discipline observed ascending the stairs, wear and tear slowing some of us
Queuing for teeth clean
Soft snoring from dark shapes, some feet in the air
Good night, loved and loving
Dirty beard, Dog of Flanders - Bouviers.

John R. June 2008

# MAUTHAUSEN

I'm sitting by the pool of the Elizabeth hotel in Singapore watching the rain fall.
I've been reading 'Singapore Diary' about life as a POW in Changi Prison and felt that now maybe it was time to write about my visit to Mauthausen concentration camp in Austria.
For years I thought it was Dachau, but descriptions that I read were not the place that I could see in my mind; also it was described as a 'holding 'camp rather than 'extermination through labour' camp as it had been described to me. Seeing an aerial photo recently of what was left of the layout I knew that this was not the camp that I had visited with my parents, brother and a guide whilst my dad was working for a well known charity.

So, what was I remembering?
I mentioned my confusion to Mum - where had we gone? What was it called? She couldn't recall the name except that it started with an 'M'; and then the name came as if it had been hiding behind the name Dachau. "Was it Mauthausen?" I asked, Mum's eyes opened wide with recognition and absolute assurance, "Yes that was it!"

I described a few scenes that I had held in my mind for many years but rarely spoken of. Were they correct? Was I remembering the place as it really was or had my childhood memory altered over the years?
My descriptions fitted her memories; we were remembering the same place, my perspective slightly altered as I was only a child. For example a very high wall as remembered by me was apparently only about 7 feet high but the places, the sights, the descriptions, were the same.
Now I could write about it.
To be doubly sure I looked up 'Mauthausen' on the Web and there it was. It was a surprising shock, so much so,
that I had to show my husband to show him that my memories were true, places I'd mentioned and described to him were there on the screen, but without much of the detail that our guide had told us all those years ago.
It became clear why I had remembered the name Dachau, it was not far away and was the holding camp before those poor souls interned there were sent on to other places for work or worse, the majority of prisoners being sent down the line to Mauthausen, primarily a labour camp which became a camp for 'extermination through labour'.

**I see Mum, Dad and my brother, but not the guide that I know was with us.**
**We are walking across a large area - grass and path, towards the camp. I feel overawed but having no understanding of what we were being brought to.**
**It was all part of Dad's work. He visited refugee camps in Austria - displaced people whose stories were repeated time and time again, he preached in Anglican churches and collected money to help them and now we were going to see one of the places where so many others had gone, never to return.**
**They themselves, the refugees, had so very little and lived in corrugated tin huts with sacking for doors, inside were the few possessions they had carried with them as they fled; but as far**

as they were concerned, they were lucky. They were alive, and even my child mind understood that. What I could not have expected was what I saw on our visit to Mauthausen that day, and my parent's reaction to it…and my reaction, even with my childish understanding. The things I saw and the feeling that it left me with, have lasted crystal clear all these years, emotions and pictures in my memory, undimmed by over 45 years.

Mauthausen - Camp for extermination through labour.

Walking towards it I was just interested, what it held was appalling.
It had been cleared but not cleaned up, no labels or photos.
It was the first time that I saw dried blood and learnt that it turns brown with age.

There is no sequence to what I remember seeing, only snapshots of areas; and the stories that the guide told to us.

A room, bedroom sized with a metal shower head in the ceiling (I remember only one but possibly there were more). A heavy metal door with a peephole in it.
The guide explained…the elderly, the weak, women and children who arrived at the camp were told that they were to have a shower. They took off their clothes, their heads were shaved (under the pretext of not allowing lice into the camp), they put down their few belongings and took off their glasses, jewellery, watches etc. They were led to the 'shower room'. The heavy metal door was closed behind them.
With bewilderment and then growing fear they heard the hiss of water coming through the pipes, but no water for the shower came through the 'shower heads'. With terror they would have smelt the gas…and realised.
The tiny glass peep hole in the door was for the guards to look through to check that all were dead before opening the door and pulling the bodies out, ready to take to the incinerators nearby.

The 'ovens', waist high from the ground, like bread making ovens from long ago. Two together, ash inside, ash on the floor. Metal 'stretchers', to pile the bodies on and slide them into the ovens to be incinerated. The guide told us that the ovens were going all day and all night every day from when it took its first victims to the day it was liberated. All day and all night burning people, as a child I was horrified. I held my Mum's hand. It was not the first time that day that I saw tears falling down her face.

Another room, small, with a gutter running to the middle

where there was a small drain hole - Mum remembers it too. Brown stains on the wall opposite the door. The guide explained - it was the measuring room. People were told they were to be measured. They were told to stand against the wall opposite the door and someone would come in to measure them. As the door closed a rifle was placed against the hole in the door and they were shot. The blood was easily swilled down the gutter into the drain.
This one is a mystery to me as I find it difficult to imagine that the soldiers would bother killing one at a time when they had so many other wholesale methods, but maybe this was early on before they became so blasé and efficient.
I would doubt my memory but Mum remembered the room and the same details.

The 'wailing wall' where men were chained, interrogated and beaten was the wall that I remember as being so very tall. In my mind's eye I can see a wall maybe 20 feet high, but in reality it was probably only about 7 feet.
Things seem so very big when you are a child.
It was standing here that for the first time in my life I remember seeing my Dad cry, tears streamed down his face as he must have realised the magnitude of what had happened here only about 15 years previously.

The stairs of Death; the stone steps, leading up from a quarry. Men carrying huge blocks up the rough carved out steps, one after the other, forced labour, men weak for lack of food, skeletal thin, trying so hard to keep their balance in the heat of the sun, the drenching rain, the biting cold of the snow, all weathers, it didn't matter to the guards as long as the job was done. And if a missed footing or fainting through hunger caused one to fall then the others went down too, like dominoes, the fall and the huge boulders causing death or fatal injuries. Some would reach the top only to be pushed over the edge whilst others looked on knowing that they might well be the next. How do men carry on in the face of such labour and fear; and how do men perpetrate it? I can only think that extreme pressure and extreme circumstances bring out the very best and the very worst of human nature in the people put into those circumstances by others.
I learnt that there are no bounds to what one human being is capable of doing to another.

I saw the operating tables and again the brown stains on the floors.
I listened in silence to what the guide told us.
Gold fillings in teeth extracted by drill or pliers - the gold to be melted down for the good of the cause, to fund arms to

continue the fight, to build more camps, to build a new, all powerful nation to crush all those who didn't fit or didn't agree with the leader and his vision for the future.
Surgical procedures tried out as experiments - no anaesthetic.
Diseases injected into healthy live people – to see what would happen.
Human skin used as lampshades.
It didn't seem real; but the silence with which my parents received this information and the gentle sadness with which it was relayed told me that it had been very real.
It had happened, to the elderly, women and men; and to children and babies.
Looking back, these memories are ones I have carried with me but have rarely spoken of, other than to say that I went there - they have seemed too big to talk of in mere conversation, but having spoken to my Mum about it, it seemed the right time to write it all down.
I'm not sure in this day and age of protecting children from anything vaguely unpleasant in life, that the things I saw in my childhood journeys during the course of my Dad's work would have been approved of. I have the feeling that I might have been offered counselling to help with the trauma of what I had seen and heard and I'm sure that my parents would have been disapproved of for exposing my brother and I to such horrors but it did me no harm.
It gave me a massive empathy with minority groups; it made me always side with the underdog; it made me intolerant of those who have much and who have no idea that there are those who have nothing; it made me see a hundred sides to any story; it made me realise that we have within us the possibility to be good or evil and that we cannot always choose; that we can be strong or weak and that neither makes us a greater or lesser human being.
It gave me a thirst to understand human nature and, if possible, to be gentle and generous of spirit to all those with whom I came in contact.
It also helped me see that my parents cared, not only about my brother and me and each other, but about all people and if they could help they would.
It was a good lesson to learn.

# Images

I studied graphic art as part of my college course back in the 1970s but have no training in photography, only a delight in seeing and photographing images that excite me.

Texture, pattern, shape, natural, man-made, real and abstract all are fascinating.
Our world is full of images that evoke feelings in all of us, I like to capture them and revisit them at my leisure.

Some of my photographs have been exhibited, many sold in card form, all of them remind me of times and places when I saw, stopped and captured a moment in my life that made my heart smile.
Jo

I started to write 'Longbarrow' some time ago and then events overtook me and I have left it for some time now. Whenever I go to Dorset I start to think about it again and have decided to dig it out and try to 'get going'.
It has two stories really and I've put two extracts in to this book. The first reminds me of a time when I worked as a Marie Curie nurse and was amazed to go t a lady who seemed to be quietly and successfully dying, alone, in her wow home, attended only be the strangers (including myself) who came and went at appointed times. She seemed unworried and accepting and in an odd sort of way it didn't seem sad, it just seemed to be what she wanted and therefore right.
Lindsay

**The woman on the bed groans softly and her breathing quickens. I put down my book and lean over to take her hand. I alter the angle of the bedside lamp so that it shines a little more directly on to her face.**
**I am her nurse. I am fifty. She is ninety three years old and now at the end of her life. I have been in this situation many times before but it never becomes routine, never loses its impact. By 'impact' I don't mean that it upsets me…it doesn't. I am not related to these people, my patients, they are not my family or even my friends but they are in my care at this most definitive time in their lives…their death.**

**How many times have I wandered slowly around their homes trying to soak up a little of what has made them as they are. I find it ceaselessly fascinating. The black and white grainy wedding photos. Young, unworldly faces squinting in to the camera, large, trailing bouquets, unflattering head dresses worn low over the brow, dresses which stop just above the ankle making the outward turned feet look overly large. Grooms in tight suits with huge button holes, gloves stretched primly over their hands, even on the hottest of days. I think I find wedding photographs the most touching, the most merciless. The contrast between the hopeful, sometimes beautiful faces and the time worn features which present themselves to me, often in suffering or misery seem endlessly shocking and impossible to believe in.**

**The woman's name is Sophie…I like that, a change from the usual Mabels and Dorises. There is no wedding photo, Sophie being a single woman, a spinster as she would have been called in other times. In fact there is very little clue to Sophie's life in this small, comfortable bungalow, one or two pictures, random groups of young people turning from their lunch in the garden, their game of tennis, to smile warily in to the camera before resuming their lives. No way of telling**

who they are, even examining each face in turn I have no way of gauging if one of these bright young women is my patient.

There is a card on the work top in the kitchen…a greetings card, perhaps this is from a niece or nephew, someone who cares. It is actually a card welcoming Sophie to her new home which is strange as I thought that the potted history in her notes said that she that she had lived there for about a year. The card reads…To Miss Davenport, We hope that you are very happy in your new home. It is signed…Anthony and Maria and underneath their names is the rubber stamped logo of a local estate agents. Well, well, so Sophie it appears had so few friends in her life that she has valued and displayed this empty PR exercise for all that time. Perhaps it was kindly meant and not just good business practise. I hope so.

I move the lamp back to its former position so that her face is not in the glare from the bulb any longer and notice that there is a tiny picture frame lying behind the lamp, one of those with a support at the back to lean on. They always get frayed and torn after a while, just as this one has. I try to stand it back up but it won't. Holding it under the lamp I can see that it is a picture of a young woman in about her twenties, seated on a horse, very upright, bursting with health and vigour, nothing wary about this smile, she looks as if she is about to break in to laughter and fling some remark at the photographer. She is wearing thick woollen jodhpurs of the old style that were wider at the thigh. They nip in her tiny waist and she wears a check shirt open at the neck. Her hands are smart in leather riding gloves and the reins are taut as if she is just managing to hold the horse back for long enough to have the photo taken. I feel sure this is Sophie. There's something about the shape of the face, the spacing of the eyes. I could be wrong but why is it here, this photo, under the lamp, by the bed, after all no other pictures are given such prominence. I feel sure it must be her. I want it to be.

Helping our children through their teenage years seems an impossible task at the time. As a mother I wanted to help, guide and support my children as much as I could; but I quickly realized that for many reasons our children tread their own often torturous paths and that all we can do is be there for them with unconditional love. That love doesn't mean always agreeing with them or necessarily approving of their choices, but it does mean holding them when they fall, listening to them when they speak and loving them regardless of anything. Jo

## The Way of our Young

Which way and how
Should we direct our young?
Which way and where
Should we guide their faltering steps?
Which path to aspire to?
Which direction to take?
How do we know what is best?

There seems no guide
No real book of how
There seems no foolproof answer
Only guesswork and hope…
And who is to blame
When their dreams go wrong?
And the young walk eyes open … to disaster.

We give them some guidelines
We show them by example
We speak of honesty and truth.
We're too hard, we're too soft
We're just muddling through
And we hope we support them enough.

But we fail them, betray them
And leave them alone,
We expect them to learn far too much
And we watch with concern
As they choose their own paths
And our hearts break with each tear they shed.

…but it was worth every anxious moment.
Now they are both grown up and it is with much love and with great pride that I watch them tread their chosen paths.

I lived and worked in London in the early '80s and the dark humour matched my mood, at the time! Lynn

## Mr. and Mrs. Average.

Bluntly, he slipped into oblivion
He turned once, flickered his eyes and fell
Such was sleep.

She on the other hand,
Knew that the beginning was near
The crack, the break
The opening
The dart of light
Which pierced her eyes
Until her aching head turned towards the clock
Such was waking.

So began another day for Mr. and Mrs. Average.

He walked, scraped his heels
Along the side of the black road
Towards the place of toil
Worn into his skin like minute
Pieces of grit,
Only mildly irritating now.

She scraped the grease away
With a tarnished knife
Listened to the fifth set of pips
On the radio that day.
Sung a little, cried for the everlasting, always, never ending,
Yet enlightened
Chores, which arise

During a day in the life of Mr and Mrs Average.

Something cracked inside.
She smiled, turned
And stood still
Till six o'clock that night.

In he came, thin lipped smile
Across the hall
Syrup rays of sun
Silhouetting his
Bulky shape against
The grubby
Frosted glass
Of
An average front door.

For the first time since morning, she moved
Only to calmly split his shoulder open
With the same tarnished knife
Grease again
Surprise glimmered in his face.

Bluntly he slipped into oblivion
He turned once
Flickered his eyes and fell.
Such was the end of a very
Unusual day, in the life of Mr.and Mrs.Average.

I banged this out very quickly because it summed up a few things I was thinking at the time! It is aimed at no one in particular (perhaps just men in general!) Lindsay

## I Want a Me (A female rant).

A cake to take? I'll bake it.
A bed unmade? I'll make it.
You mowed the lawn? I'll rake it.
An orgasm? I'll fake it.

I want a me.

I'll run our business, yours and mine
Send out all the bills on time
See employees when they whine
So you can leave me, what a crime!

I want a me.

A home to run? I'll do it.
A casserole? I'll stew it.
Fish out of date? I threw it.
Forgot to iron? You blew it.

I want a me.

The cupboard's full of ironed sheets,
Clothes on rails all folds and pleats
Every room is fresh and neat
Don't leave your work boots on that seat!

I want a me.

You tell me that I'm never wrong
And make it sound a two edged song
For just one thing I simply long,

A Me!

*You know when you are first in love and the object of your desire goes away -it's your first physical parting and you ache for their return -as well as loving the anticipation of it - I really imagined the snowy landscapes where John was skiing and how he looked in his salopettes!!!* Lynn 1986

## Where You Are

Do the trees whisper
Where you are?
Does the snow glisten blue at night?
Do the steep flanks of the valleys
Gasp at dawn and glow
With the rose morning light?

Are there smiling faces
Where you are?
Do you move easily with friends
And gracefully turn
For a tingling descent?
Where the air
Cold caresses and exhilarates you
Where you are?

Here the rain and colours soft
Have not shocked the senses
Nor the friendly faces
And deep talk.

I have moved in a space
Amused
Confused
And aching for the things
Where you are.

Each winter, usually January or February, Lynn and Lindsay organise an evening of entertainment at Spooner Row church (Holy Trinity) which is called Gloombusters. The first one was in 2003.

It started because, although they both love to sing they enjoy doing it just for themselves or a few friends rather than in a more formal way, so they held Gloombusters as a 'one off" party and it has since become an annual event. The format is chaotic and informal and is really about friendship and having a laugh more than anything else. The proceeds from the donations are divided between the church, the Village Hall and a local charity which changes each year. Entrance is free and by invitation only - we certainly wouldn't expect our friends to buy a ticket in order to suffer quite that much! They donate generously, clap and cheer wildly, regardless of content and the whole thing gives us great pleasure.

One year a ghost story was split in to episodes throughout the evening. There was a truly scary 'dead bride' and the effect in the church when all the lights and the overhead heaters were switched off enhanced the drama by means of such an instant and bone killing chill that the audience felt the dead had indeed arisen and returned to haunt them on 'Gloombuster's Eve'! Lindsay.

# The Return of Lydia.

I well remember that night. It was the night I had arranged to meet Lydia, my dearest Lydia. I felt excited and not a little anxious; such a long time since I had seen my love – a full year in fact.
It also stays well in my mind because, of course, it was Gloombuster's eve, a night when anything might happen – and often does my friends.

I had taken the Bunwell Road that evening and though it was dark when I set off there had been a full, clear moon casting its light over the jagged spines of the hedgerows and the frosted fields but by the time I reached the cross roads at the Three Boars it had long been blotted out by great swathes of blanketing cloud. I could almost reach out and touch the blackness of the night and felt the sharp edge of snow threatening in the air.

I can tell you I was mighty glad to see the light softly beaming from the window of that most delightful hostelry and to hear the sound of voices raised in talk and laughter which rose to a great burst of song as I pushed open the heavy door and went thankfully in to the snug.

Anthony is a most genial host and I was pleased to see his open friendly countenance and to smell the good, homely aroma of baking pies which wheedles its way out of the kitchen when the landlady, Ruth, is at her range.

It's a strong man can resist the smell of baking but I well knew that time was short so I took up the offer of a place by the glowing grate and raising my coat tails to better feel the warmth, I accepted a proffered flagon of warmed ale and refused, reluctantly to sit down at the long oak table where my fellow men were already addressing a great pie with a golden crust which had broken to release a stream of gravy thick with succulent meats. Although I say I was reluctant in my refusing of a repast – yet it was no real hardship because my appetite was over shadowed, nay defeated by the knowledge that I would soon hold my own dear Lydia once more in my arms.

The old school clock over the hearth chimed the half hour – 10.30, this would not do. I downed the last of my good ale, surrendered my place by the comforting coals to a poor soul newly arrived whose very whiskers appeared stiff with frost and after calling a goodnight to the landlord and his wife, I let myself out and was instantly seized in to the icy black grip of the night.

As I stepped on to the silent crossroad I could make out in the distance the soft glow of the level crossing lanterns at Spooner Row Station. The light was diffused in the darkness but nonetheless it gave some comfort as I turned my face towards the church. I entered the gateway and made my way up the path.

Despite the intense darkness I could just make out the shape of the ancient bell hanging high above me on the southern end of the church and the silvery grey outlines of the tomb stones leaning at the angles wrought by time and weather.
'How long' I wondered fleetingly, 'before I take my place amongst those beckoning stones'?
This was thankfully but a passing thought as my mind was all but fully occupied with happier expectations. An owl hooted high in the trees around the graveyard and the church cat sidled against my legs causing me to start and cry out. I then felt foolish and looked quickly round but no man was there to hear me – only the dead!
My great coat pocket was all but dragged out of shape by the solid and reassuring weight of the great church key which I had made sure of obtaining earlier that evening from the good wife Rosemarie who tended so carefully to the care and upkeep of the church. She herself had been busy about the

parish that afternoon but her daughter, the fair maid Kerrie, soon to be wed to her sweetheart Mark at the nearby Abbey had called at my cottage door to leave me the key and pass a few pleasant moments in conversation ; a comely lass! I could envy her intended if my heart wasn't long promised elsewhere. I inserted the key in to the ancient lock and with much protesting and groaning it turned and the door swung open allowing me in to the still darkness of the church.
Although I felt comforted, as always, in the church at Spooner Row, yet it was a chilly welcome at that January time of the year. The stone floor offered up no warmth, the blessed simplicity of the vaulted ceiling sent me no heat and yet, as ever in this holy place I felt as if I had returned home after a long and wearisome journey.
I sensed around me in the chill night air echoes of familiar and much loved sounds, the mellow fluting of the Recorder Group who met there on Wednesday evenings to fill the little church with their ancient Sarabandes, Galliards and gay Pavanes. I could see them in my mind's eye; John, Andrew, Francis, all good men and true with Dame Katherine underlining their music with her steady ground bass, keeping the group in order when their male exuberance threatened to overwhelm them.
Then again I heard the echoes of honest village voices raised in song on bright summer Sundays, at Harvest Suppers and in the age-old carols at Christmastide. At all these festivals good wife Rosemarie would be found in the little kitchen stirring simmering cauldrons of mulled wine, cutting cheeses for the Harvest board and generally helping the atmosphere of conviviality and good cheer.
Suddenly I heard the strains of the little pipe organ, and quite thought that my mind was bringing to me treasured memories of happy hours spent listening to the choir master, Philip, who lives close by in Wymondham, and has played the organ at Spooner Row for many a year (though he looks but yet a boy). The choir master and his wife, Mistress Josephine have long been friends. Many's the evening we have sat, Philip and I, locked in combat over the chess board while his wife Josephine refreshes our palates and delights our eyes with her presence.
I listened again and whirled round from my place at the altar step to find to my intense delight that it was not my mind tricking me into imaginings of gentle music but no, it was my fair Lydia, my own, my love, who had come softly in to that darkened church, had lit a flickering candle to shed its light over the yellowing keys and in the same action illuminated her face for my grateful eyes to see.
I stood as if fixed to the cold flag stones. My Lydia was as

beautiful as ever, the fair beauty who had long reigned in my mind. I think I called her name though I cannot be sure but she turned to face me, her hands falling from the keys and yet, although I barely noticed then, the music continued, the keys depressed as if still feeling the touch of her slender fingers. She came to me then, her silvery hair floating like a mist about her face, the grey of her eyes and the gentle rose of her lips, striking me anew with their beauty. She spoke my name, softly as a sigh on the night air and I folded her in my arms, light as thistledown, gentle as a morning mist, her gown of shimmering blue gathered in soft folds as if to protect her from the night.

We walked as we have done every year, down the aisle towards the great door. Lydia lifted that heavy protesting latch at a touch of her gentle hand and led me through the darkness which seemed to lighten and glow as we walked.
We reached the far, North corner of the churchyard, as I knew and dreaded we would. My Lydia turned as before, to face me, smiled and raised one arm high in the air as blessing and farewell and, as I ran forward, calling to her, begging her to stay, she stepped lightly on to the grassy mound at the foot of the tall Celtic cross marked with the name, Lydia Ravenhurst and vanished even as I watched.

I should be better able to bear these meetings or else should stay at home, close by my cottage fire but still each year I am drawn to meet my fate on Gloombuster's Eve.

*Getting older, divas, fragile self confidence and a love of theatre led to this one (other than that - can't remember).*
*Lynn 1980s*

## Supernova

She shook slightly, mainly because of the damp
And the cramp in her leg
Was irritating.

Look in the mirror
And at the assorted sizes
Shapes, colours of pots and
Make up….plain woman

Nervously smoothing false
Colour, tone and character
Across the lined skin
Loose now, but they are too far away to see the lines.

In the 1700s, wasn't there a supernova
In the constellation Cassiopeia, the Queen….
Which grew to such
Amazing intensity that it
Could be seen when
The sun itself was in the sky?

The costume now
Gently caressing the
Very slightly sagging frame
With its gentle folds of whiteness,
Soon to be transformed.

The supernova faded
As quickly as it came, in astronomical terms,
But supernovas have this tendency…
It's life.

Through the ropes and shaking scenery
Damp with the heat of people and dusty footlights -
Sweet Desdemona Supernova, scintillate well tonight
For in that appreciative audience (though they still admit to being culture hungry)
There is one less person than there was the night before.

When a marriage ends it can be very hard to believe that love and happiness can ever be in your life again. or that you even deserve such gifts. These four poems, among others, written over the span of a year show how I was given that chance by the man who I am proud to call my husband.  Jo

# Who?

Who is this man who quietly sits
And listens without a word?
Who holds me close and doesn't judge
Regardless of what I've done.

Who is this man who gently talks
In a voice as soft as rain?
Who strokes my hair and holds my hand
And seems as if he cares?

Who is this man who talks with me
About his life and times?
Who smiles and cries and laughs and sighs
And seems to understand.

# YOU

You make me feel calm
You make me feel warm
You make me want to laugh

You make me feel joy
You make me feel peace
You've opened up my heart.

# YOU

A warm laugh bubbles and overflows
A smile blossoms in my eyes
A peace soaks into my heart
I am with you.

# I Can

I can talk with you
Laugh with you,
Dance with you
And play.

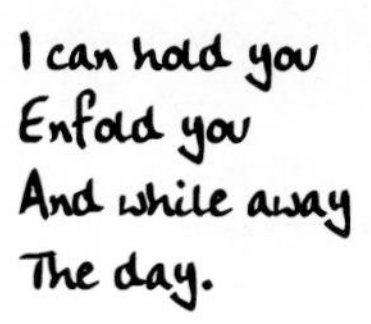

I can hold you
Enfold you
And while away
The day.

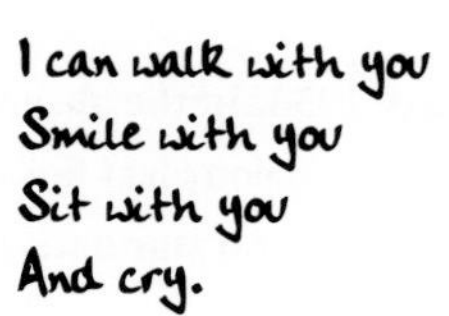

I can walk with you
Smile with you
Sit with you
And cry.

I can kiss you
Caress you
And hold you
As we fly.

## EARTH

Lynn

Hello friends from galaxy 1954. In the absence of my boss, I have been asked to respond to your last few questions prior to your visit to the UK, on Earth, on star date 24 04 2008.

These are a few, very idiosyncratic views of life on Earth- in a nutshell; they may be of no use to you whatsoever, but given that I am an ordinary sort of female in middle years, of middling intelligence and living in the middle latitudes....it could be said that I am an average sort of person. These are things, which could be seen as important in understanding us.
Firstly, there's a connectedness in everything, so if we start with the EARTH we will end up back there.
'Earth to Earth'.
This will only cease, as you well know, when the sun comes to the end of its life and grows to a red super giant and cooks the planets in our solar system.
That's why the Earth can be impossibly beautiful...because ALL GOOD THINGS COME TO AN END.
It's especially important to note the resonance in everything, for example, bird song.
Layers of it, its intricate music, in the spring.
Spring???
We have seasons in our latitudes. The yearning for the next one always means that you are nostalgic for the one before... e.g. yearning for spring, but remembering a winter fire in your home with your dog snoring at your feet.
Dogs???
Are fantastic (...as are many animals). They love you and are loyal to you for very little in return. They make you feel ok about yourself, in fact give you a reason to carry on when it all gets a bit difficult with other humans.

**Other humans???**
**You can be loved by other humans. The safest receptacle for love is friendship. There are lots of different loves.....BUT the one that has caused all the great artists to deepen and widen their subjects and their colours and all the great wordsmiths to expand...is PASSION!**
**Passion???**
**If it's passion...it can all get a bit messy and risks are taken. Friendship means that we do things for OTHER people, not just ourselves...no matter what. Passion tends to be more selfish...but reminds us of spring and birdsong. Love now, is different again. There's some love that just always was and always will be...like you have for someone who was there when you were born and even if they die they're always with you. They make you happy.**
**Happy???**
**When you are happy, you sometimes laugh and the time (seconds, minutes etc....earth time) goes VERY fast. If you are miserable and can't open your mind to anything other than PROBLEMS, it goes VERY slowly.**
**Time???**
**Time is running out for many people. We are lucky, where we live. Enough to eat. Education. Little danger.**
**Danger???**
**In some places people want to kill each other because someone has a different set of beliefs than they do or have something that they want or they have terrible diseases which we could afford to help them cure, but we don't because they are not our people. The others, who ARE our people, work hard to raise money to cure people in those other places!!! This is called COMPASSION and isn't very popular here at the moment. Some very young people who don't want to die get killed and then in other places, very old or sick people who do want to die aren't allowed to and LOADS of money is spent on curing diseases to make us live longer and longer. Sometimes in these places though, people show a thing called bravery which is a bit like love.**
**Bravery???**
**They will sacrifice their lives for others who need the help or put things right that they believe in. Sometimes parents are very brave for their children and sometimes children are very brave for their parents...which is very different.**
**People on the whole are very muddled up. They put people in charge of their countries that they 'elect' as 'people who know what's best' and then they spend the next years complaining about them. Ho Hum!**
**People who don't have too much, but JUST ENOUGH tend to be the ones who can see the beauty in the Earth. These are**

the ones it's worth getting to know as they make 'life worth living'. They can love the blue of the sky, trees, and the sea... the impossible sea. How can something so dangerous be so beautiful? There's a lot of it round us here in our country. Anyway, must go and drive home on a clogged road, only to return tomorrow!

However, we think you'll get on rather well here. Most people will be very interested in when and why you moved away and how you saved all the animals that are now extinct here...how you protected the lungs of your planet by planting more rain forests. How you consistently feel ok about yourselves and create very beautiful art and music and never drop litter and never fight.

Weren't greedy.

Used your resources wisely.

Anyway, if we are interconnected, us and you...you may be able to help us, because I fear the Earth is IMPOSSIBLY beautiful...It will come to an end....and I hope if we meet, maybe we can arrange a job swap!

Bye for now.

This is the second extract from the 'work in progress' (slow progress!) which I will probably call 'Longbarrow' if I ever get it finished!
Lindsay

The door opened and Monika stood there, cracklingly clean blue jeans, striped cotton shirt collar jutting out from a cream pullover and a face so open and glowing with health that it made me feel like a very small, pale mouse, a librarian perhaps, definitely someone who burrowed indoors for a living. Her eyes were clear and she had tawny hair, shining in strong auburn waves with just the odd piece of chaff or something sticking to it in places. Behind her, hand extended, face beaming, was James, relaxed looking, in easy chunky sort of clothes, large feet encased in thick woollen socks, no shoes or slippers, at home and comfortable to be there.
Monika beamed a welcome, stepped back heavily on to James' woolly foot then told him to "get out of the bloody way then" if he wasn't going to get dressed properly.
He seemed quite unabashed and without quite knowing how it happened, we found ourselves in a small hallway off the kitchen where we paused while Monika went through a door to one side and proceeded to shout in no uncertain terms at what I took to be some more of the dogs that we had already met in the kitchen.
"Out! I told you earlier that I wanted this room clean and clear" (clear ended in a long soft Somerset burr that I hadn't noticed before) " Get off that sofa, come on you buggers, get outside the lot of you".

I stood back, waiting for a rush of animals and was promptly introduced, one by one to four large, pale, resigned looking teenagers who loped in to the hall, muttered "Hi" when forced to it and reluctantly vanished in to the kitchen on the way to 'make themselves useful outside',
"And don't stop in the kitchen and eat all the bread and jam or I'll kill you!" I imagined that she didn't mean this literally but wouldn't have been surprised if she had!
We turned back to the door and a small, bristly Jack Russell trotted sedately out, confident of it position, its right to be there. Monika swooped down and picked it up.
"And this is my darling Jigger, he's a good boy isn't he", this to Jigger, who definitely agreed and licked her nose and chin with enthusiasm. She set him down gently and he trotted importantly through to the kitchen where I guess he could have eaten all the bread and jam in the house if he had felt inclined to.

Monika ushered us in to the little room, pulling at rugs and cushions and keeping up a torrent of half welcoming, half complaining talk, most of it clearly and loudly aimed at the teenagers who could be heard, quite distinctly, banging cupboard doors and rustling bread bags in the kitchen.
"Why do I bother, why do I bother?" she gazed round at us as if expecting an answer and then pushed the door to with her foot and dropped down in to an armchair.
James padded towards a chair over by the window and was stopped midway by Monika who gave him a list of instructions about coffee which had nearly perked, sausage rolls which would burn at any moment, bloody kids who should be forced out of the kitchen while there was any food left at all and made to clear up the barn, "like they have promised to do since that last fracas with Fred Jobbins and his mates.". She raised her eyebrows so high when she said this that they virtually disappeared in to her hair line and gave us a very knowing look but offered no explanation whatever so we let it pass and continued to float on the tide of her chatter and good humour. James disappeared and clattered about in the kitchen and Monika finally settled down and asked about our plans and where were we living while we converted the house and generally seemed fascinated with all that we had to say.
She had the effect always of making life seem far more 'alive' than it could possibly be..jokes were funnier, sadnesses sadder, it usually left us kind of battered but energised.
We spent hours in their company that afternoon, we drank enough coffee to float a battleship, and I was bursting to go to the loo but felt I didn't want to break the spell of the laughter and the seeming intimacy of the moment. Jack and I, I suppose, weren't used to such easy, welcoming familiarity, such generosity and friendship on so casual a basis. Was it the 'country way' or just the 'Monika way'? A bit of both I suspect.
It was quite dusky by the time we wandered back down our drive and let ourselves in at the back door. The house seemed all the colder and gloomier for its comparison with the afternoon which seemed to glow in our minds.
"Well" said Jack, "do you see what I mean about Monika?"

"I certainly do" I smiled "Aren't we lucky to have them as neighbours. She asked if I'd like to ride out with her."

"You can't ride" said Jack, a little abruptly I thought. (I guess he considered Monika rather his territory).

"She said she would teach me if I wanted."

"And will you have a go? I thought it scared you that time when we both tried before."

"If she offers I think I will," I said.
I had a feeling it might be different with Monika.

I don't write poetry. My friends do and so I am able to enjoy theirs. The following is put in at their request and is the nearest thing to a love poem that I am ever likely to produce. (I don't know why - 'Stuffy' Dowding, my husband said it was a nickname at school, anyhow, it refers to him - (or his legs at any rate!)
Lindsay

**Stuffy Dowding's got good legs Miss**
**Saw them by the rugby pitch.**
**Sneaked a look while he was changing**
**'Till the Head came, Life's a bitch!**

**When he pulls those rugby socks up**
**Snug and warm they fit the knee**
**I can only gaze in wonder**
**Wishing that those socks were me!**

(I think there were more verses, fortunately they have not survived.)

I always like the spring and can't wait for its arrival after winter. I'd just met John and was first in love and very tuned in to the early spring. He went away skiing (see 'Where You Are' written at the same time) and I was missing him. I went out cycling around the north Norfolk lanes and the sensuality of the land and the birdsong inspired me.

Lynn 1986

## Spring

The sun comes out in March
Sometimes
(After the long cold winter weeks)
With ferocious gaiety,
Sparring with the clouds
To touch with light
And caress
The curves and lifts of the fields
Where they undulate towards
The warmth.
Every place hums, but ceases only
To listen………
To the gusts and thrusts
Of the fickle wind.

The land opens its lazy hand to the spring
And the first Skylark sings.

We decided to write down, quickly, without planning, what we each feel we have gained from knowing the other two. We weren't allowed to change anything. Here they are:

**Jo**

Sense of peace
Outlet for literary passion
Unexpected friendship
Acceptance

**Lindsay**

Humility
The need to show kindness
Fun
Release of imagination.

**Lynn**

Madness
Creativity
Warmth
Laughter
Wickedness

**The wonder of women.**